The Cell Block Presents...

The BASic Fundamentals of The Game

Published by: The Cell Block™

The Cell Block
P.O. Box 212
Folsom, CA 95763

www.thecellblock.net

Copyright © 2014 by Maurice Vasquez

Cover Design: Mike Enemigo

Send comments, reviews, interview and business inquiries to:
thecellblock@mail.com

All rights reserved. This book may not be reproduced in whole or in part without written permission from the publisher, except by a reviewer who may quote brief passages in a review; nor may any part of this book be reproduced, stored in retrieval system, or transmitted in any form or by any means, electronic, mechanical, photocopying, recording, or other, without written permission from the publisher.

Acknowledgements

Traditionally authors start off their work by thanking their editors and publishers…This book is no exception, so let me first express my genuine gratitude to The Cell Block! Not only for dispensing their enormous assistance and expertise during the construction of this project, but also for having the courage to publish such a raw authentic illustration of truth that many may interpret as narcissistic grandiosity.

Furthermore, I immensely appreciate the faith and confidence you demonstrated by trusting in and interpreting my artistic vision so that it could manifest into what we wanted to accomplish.

I say "we" because although these are my words, spoken from the convictions of my principles and personal experiences, it was certainly not just me who invested their time and energy into the literary venture.

My lil bruh Mike Enemigo! I'm astounded at how intuitive and intricate your creative genius is. Literally playboy, seldom am I granted the privilege of encountering someone who truly fucken gets it! You understood what I articulated wanting to do and shared your innovative ideas to maximize the magnitude of this incredibly important epistle that I have written for all those interacting within the threshold of The Game.

Yo Rowdy! You were right here while I was writing, brainstorming, envisioning, improvising, contemplating, processing, planning, executing, and prophesying; so you know firsthand the hard work and passion that went into this. Your input and feedback was appreciated as well playboy.

To all my goons out there grindin', goin' hard n' getting' it!..

For all my young thugs conquering and capitalizing!.. To my loyal disciples devoted and dedicated to their performance of duties!..

All you players in The Game fully committed to the longevity and prosperity of our lifestyle! This one is for all of you! The Game is ours!.. There are no time outs! We get no half times! For us, there is no spring break! No Christmas vacation. No sick leave! No time off for good behavior! No out for the season due to a fucken injury! If we get hurt while on the field or on the job, we get no workman's comp or disability! We gotta grit our teeth and go even harder!

That means no sleepin' on the fucken job! The higher the altitude the more difficult it is to breath. Keep raising those standards so that those around us have to walk on their tip toes in order for them not to choke!

And to all you game deficient imposters, yeah this is for you bitch made mutha fuckas too. Til now, you've been relying on the excuses of your ignorance and confusion to serve as an explanation of why you're so fucken stagnant! Unfortunate for you, that shenanigans will no longer work. For many of you, you are so far behind that it's impossible for you to catch up. The word is now out there for the Game to see! The Game Guru MAS BAS has spoken; and I approve this message. Paid for and endorsed by advocates of truth!

Personal Introduction

I am loyally devoted to The Game. So much so that it can even be considered an obsession. I have mastered my method, hence, becoming a mentor to many players whom aspire to conquer the difficulties which I've surmounted. I am sought out by other players for the knowledge which I've acquired through practice and experience. I am properly placed on an elevated plateau among those who lead and serve The Game. However, one of many aspects that makes me extraordinarily unique, is that unlike my predecessors whom sat at the top of the hill strategically managing things from afar, out of harm's way, I prefer being right here on the frontline of the battlefield, engaged in hand to hand combat, getting my hands dirty. The easy way of doing something has never been my way of getting the job done. That does not imply that I enjoy making things more difficult for myself than they already are. What I mean is that I am constantly faced with difficult situations which require hard work and dedication to resolve, and I have never been one who is willing to neglect doing whatever the fuck is necessary to fulfill my duties. I feel a deep responsibility for The Game. I often hear muthafuckers saying that *It's just business, it's nothing personal*. It's a problem to think like that. My involvement in The Game has always been a very personal process, so to me, it's *all* personal! How can it not be? Think about it. If something personally affects me or those I care for, how the fuck is it *not* personal?!

To me, that cliché is some of the stupidest shit I've ever heard. The Game is too complex for us to examine the evidence on every issue in which we need to make up our minds. We live in a world filled with "purported experts." We are bombarded with many different judgments, opinions, clichés, and assumptions. We need the tools to judge among them, so we need to find the experts of The Game whom we can trust; players who have demonstrated that they have the knowledge and expertise, the objectivity and integrity to provide reliable guidance.

Most players I know are skeptics who insist on objective proof before something is believed; what to inculcate seems to be at the root of this problem. If each generation of up-and-coming players are being taught the same unsuccessful, contradictory methods that he learned growing up in The Game before actually being able to evaluate them, then as a society we are contributing toward the catastrophe that has plagued The Game, hence, producing imposters who might have had a chance to become a factor had he been taught The BASic Fundamentals of The Game.

Although we are inclined to believe that our opinions and personal views of The Game are objective because it is generally consistent with that of our immediate surroundings, what our opinions actually contain is a perception that's reflected by that of what we "believe" is accurate. So if we are surrounded by inaccuracies and inconsistencies, understandably we are susceptible to *believing* that it's a representation of our reality (which is outlandish and couldn't be further from the truth).

It is this fact that makes me look in bewilderment at the actions of others who identify themselves as players, yet conduct an image contrary to it. Many of us learned our general beliefs before we were able to evaluate them. The beliefs we hold today which were learned when we were kids are uninformed, unquestioned beliefs. We did not have the ability to examine what we were being taught, nor the capacity to reject or accept those teachings.

Those who influenced us when we were growing up are who reflect the beliefs of our culture. When we learn to "believe" before we learn to "think" we are vulnerable because an empty mind does not have the capacity to understand what it should nor shouldn't believe. This conundrum is constantly epitomized in observing the going-on of The Game. One of the many mistakes I see is the way that some people thrive on past experiences to the point they remain stuck in the past. Although your personal history is important, it can be detrimental if it hinders your ability to be productive. Past insights, past innovation, past creativity, past accomplishments are only relevant if you are still producing favorable results. What are you accomplishing *now*? What are you accumulating *now*? What is your repertoire of techniques? In what way are you contributing toward The Game *now*? You can't keep doing the same thing and expect it to keep working. You have to do something different in order to progress; but the really hard question is *what is it*? Well, first of all you must have a goal; you must know what you want to be, where you want to go, and what you want to do. Part of my enormous responsibility as a Mac is helping players get the best from The Game and learn how to maximize their potential so that they are able to live with its arduous experiences and succeed in a way that is both effective and creative. In order for his to happen, however, a player has to have the intuitive insight and understanding concerning who he is, what he actually wants, and most importantly what he can do!

I'm fascinated by the amazing things a player can accomplish with the right guidance. There are certain principles involved in The Game that can release the potential to do something astounding. I have mentored many players in The Game who have become factors, and who are exemplary in all facets. Their strong personal values have impelled them to always do right by the laws of The Game regardless of the circumstances. That's not to say there haven't been problems along the way. There will always be problems. If you don't have any problems occurring, you have absolutely nothing going on in your life. When you have a problem, you are given an opportunity to solve it. Whether you realize it or not, opportunities give you the advantage. You will eventually realize that shit is not as complicated as you first speculated. Solving problems builds creativity and creativity is a key component to intellectual insight. Remember; without problems there would be no progress!

I felt that it was important for me to come forward with this work. I'm outlining the dynamics and principles to encourage all players to put them in perspective and incorporate them into their game plan. Its purpose is to persuade all participants of The Game to practice properly. I've been contemplating a plan on how best to get the word out to relate this very important message. What started out as an open letter, became this masterpiece of a book that I'm constructing for all those who aspire to put their player priorities in perspective.

My name is well known in The Game and my reputation is revered. My priority has never been to be liked, but to speak the truth and maintain a strong level of consistency in my convictions. In doing so, inevitably I have often endured negative reactions which at times resulted in violence. (In fact, as I'm writing this introduction, I'm here in CCI Tehachapi Security Housing Unit [solitary confinement] finishing up the final few months of a 3-year SHU term I received as a result of doing the paso doble on some schmuck's face plate.) My approach is so powerfully effective that, although it has offended many, it has won me a loyal following of players whose lives I've changed dramatically.

I encourage all players to authentically express what you think and feel! Be willing to confront inconsistencies and be prepared to deal with whatever the fuck comes your way as a result of it. In order to do so you must know what the fuck you're talking about. If you don't know what you're talking about then you're not talking about anything. Know your strong points as well as your weak points so you know where best to apply your abilities. My mind is constantly working on ways of producing new ideas. I have innovation and imagination, and I'm progressive. The very fact that I've achieved the manifestation of this literary work from right here where I have no phone access, no internet services, and everything I do is highly scrutinized, attests to what I'm articulating in regards to what remarkable things can be achieved by thinking outside the block! And get this, the Company that's publishing this "The Cell Block," is owned and operated by Mike Enemigo; a certified player in The Game whom I've mentored for many years. I first encountered him over 15 years ago and I recognized then he had a gift that could be cultivated with the right influences. To see his success is a clear indication of what the fuck I'm conveying!

I'm giving all players an opportunity to ponder my ideas, familiarize themselves with my concepts, learn my language and perceive my logic. Upon grasping the quintessential components of my character, I will establish a connection with my audience.

Before I begin, allow me to ask you this:
- ✓ What does The Game mean to you?
- ✓ What does the term "player" mean to you?
- ✓ What do you believe in?

- ✓ What do you stand for?
- ✓ What are your goals and objectives?
- ✓ What do you wish to accomplish in the game?

Upon pondering these simple yet important questions, some may realize they know a lot less than they think they do. Rather than wasting time elaborating on the thinking of others, I'm addressing key questions by examining the problem and providing my concepts to assist you in dealing with it. I chose this approach as a way of encouraging you to take the time to evaluate my concepts and think about the problems yourself. I'm attempting to assemble and interrelate what I perceive to be essential information that will help all those who study my beliefs.

When a group of players interact and converses with one another on an intellectual level you will recognize that something phenomenal occurs. While they are conversing, the atmosphere suddenly changes. As each player shares his insight and provides his input, the topic of discussion accumulates strength and becomes the motivating factor that inspires a higher level of understanding which could not have been achieved individually.

The vision that I'm eloquently describing for your mind to perceive is the epitome of what I have created for you. With that said; allow me to now present you with "The BASic

Fundamentals of The Game," an epistle from Mac BAS.

The game guru,

Lifestyle expert,

Mac BAS

The following is an original masterpiece written for the one and only true love of my life.

THE GAME

To me you're naughty and nasty, sophisticated and classy, lavish and flashy. You flourish in fame, so you stay lookin' jazzy.

You've got that platinum complexion, success is your obsession, you're a gift from God, so you're my heavenly blessin'.

You're bossy yet modest, you're flawless, a mythical Goddess. You keep me on point, 'cause you know I go the hardest!

You're beautiful and educated, down for me and dedicated, wanted by most men, so from women you're highly hated.

You're a woman of essence, you stand out in a crowd, you keep your head high, you're strong and you're proud.

You're confident and relentless, you're my gorgeous princess. I know I can rely on you, 'cause you're completely with da bidness.

You're the love of my life, my dearly devoted dame, you're my religion and faith; you are…THE GAME.

You're draped in diamonds; you enjoy winin' and dinin', you love the way I go get it when I'm grittin' and grindin'!

You're sensual, invincible, dependable; admirable, honorable, incredible. A lady of mystery, so inculcated in history, you're the only one who gets me!

Narcissistic, arrogant and conceited, yet you're lovelier than a rose. You keep me physically fitted, from my head to my toes.

You're very ambitious, that's why I made you my misses. Your kisses…are smoother than oil, you're trustworthy and loyal; you're royal.

I live for you… I'll kill for you… I'll die for you.

I'll never use your name in vain, my dearly devoted dame. You're my religion and faith, you are…THE GAME

By Maurice "Mac BAS" Vasquez

CONTENTS

The Movement

Get Your Shit Together

Hollywood Extras

Visualizing Success

The Player Process

Crash-Test Dummies

Formulate Your Game Plan

The Right Way

The Law of THE GAME

THE MOVEMENT

"You can't possibly understand the physics of the game if you don't understand the mathematics of the movement.
— Mac BAS

Over the course of the past ten years, I have encountered a great number of individuals who claim to be players in The Game, yet have absolutely no clue of the BASic fundamentals that are required to be considered an actual participant of this lifestyle. I've come to the realization that it is my responsibility to provide some essential clarification as to what actually constitutes a true player.

You see, just because a person identifies himself as a player or has aspirations to be one, certainly does not mean that he is. There is not a place that exists where someone can go and audition or enroll in a course to become a player, nor is there an individual person whom has the authority to ever approach someone and provide an invitation to participate in the going-ons of The Game. It does not work like that. Nothing worthwhile can manifest instantaneously. If that were the case, everyone would be doing something phenomenal. For instance, when someone aspires to become a lawyer, they can't just show up at the courthouse one day with briefcase in hand thinking he's going to be able to waltz his stupid ass into a court proceeding, wanting to represent a defendant who's being tried on criminal charges. Can you imagine if that were the case? Well, in many ways, the equivalent of this hypothetical scenario is actually occurring within the element of The Game. You have incompetent imposters infiltrating the threshold of The Lifestyle, portraying to be factors, when in fact they are oblivious of the way the inner dynamics of The Game operate -- much like one would have no way of truly understanding the law unless he or she invested a reasonable amount of time researching and studying it.

Take a moment to ponder this...

In terms of becoming a lawyer, you would first have to complete high school or the general education equivalent thereof. Your next endeavor would require attending college for a minimum of four years to attain a bachelor degree in Criminal Studies. Then, depending on your score when taking the LSAT (Law School Admittance Test), what law school will accept you will be determined. Once you are accepted into a law school, you still have to complete three to four years of constant schooling and studying until you'd complete all that is required to be eligible to take the State Bar exam.

Do the math: that's seven years of consistent studies after graduating high school! Let that resonate for a moment....

I'm not insinuating that it will take a minimum of seven years to be a certified player; however, the same concept applies. What I'm emphasizing is that it takes time to achieve the goal of being acknowledged as a true player.

The purpose of this epistle is to encourage you, the reader, to challenge yourself. If you consider yourself a participant of this lifestyle, whose knowledge were you the recipient of? Who were you mentored by? What goals has your mentor accomplished? Who are your mentor's colleagues? What were your mentor's methods of teaching? What were your methods of learning? Did you persistently raise significant questions that required elaborate and detailed answers? Did you engage in dialogue regarding BASic purpose and values? I ask because you can only learn the true purpose and values inculcated within The Game from a true player whom has authentic expertise.

I'm raising a very important issue and insisting that each and every individual who believes himself to be a player, take a good look at himself and evaluate his interactions and realistically assess his circumstances, so that he can honestly reflect on what attributing factors he has attributed toward the prosperity and success of The Game. Keep in mind that the conventional and traditional ways of thinking are obsolete. You can't possibly understand the truth of The Game by relying on the tradition or following the unsuccessful, fruitless method of "conventional" wisdom. You must think in terms of productivity! You must think in terms of prosperity! You must think in terms of success! The mundane mentality encourages schmucks to remain awake, aware and alert. I challenge you to relinquish the habitual ways of doing it all wrong, and instead, do the right thing by finding ways to arise, aspire, and assert! Ask yourself... What are you good at? Where do you flourish? Where do you excel? What can you do to become superb at whatever skill you have? What can you do to stimulate ideas that will produce the required determination to accomplish your goals and be efficient in your performance?

I only speak from the convictions of my personal experiences. I don't provide insight based on speculation and assumption. Everything that I eloquently articulate, yet emphasize for you, the reader, is in fact my reality....

This missive is my method of interrogating and enticing you to analyze your sense of self-understanding so that you can draw on your own conclusion. We are not sharing dialogue. I'm using this book as that of a vessel to transport my monologue from right here where I'm at, to wherever you may be. While you read my words, allow the truth of my philosophizing to emerge from these pages, and perhaps inspire you to evaluate your actions and decide whether or not you need to consider alternatives.

For me, there is no alternative. I did not choose The Game; The Game chose me. Hence, I dedicated my life to it. I have long surpassed the admirable level of a player and have reached the elevated plateau of a Mac; thus, my reputation speaks for itself. I have earned my legendary status in The Game and I continue to be demonstrative in my actions, epitomizing the true definition of a Mac to the masses of all players in The Game. This lifestyle is certainly not something that I do. This is not a passing fancy, nor a temporary transition. This is who the fuck I am. I live, breath, and bleed this movement.

Do I have your attention yet?

If you are not motivated by my monologue, then let me convey some absolute truth: This is not for you. Therefore, let me make the decision for you that you've been personally battling within the realm of your subconscious mind: Give up! Quit! Let go! Step back! For if you continue to lie to yourself; trust me when I tell you the truth *will* eventually emerge.... It *always* does.

See, truth is like water. It's pure; it's transparent; it's powerful. It's absolute! Truth also inspires; unifies; rejuvenates; motivates - it gives life! But it can also take it away.... So I instruct you to keep it real with yourself. You may be able to convince others around you of your "authenticity" because they too lack the BASic fundamentals, but believe me when I tell you that there are those of us who can spot an imposter from a mile away. You may be able to memorize the lines from your script or recite the lyrics and dance to the beat of your favorite song; but when it comes down to performing with precision during the precarious positions of adversity, you'll need a fucking stunt double!

Oil becomes sludge in the midst of murky waters. It floats to the top and drifts in whatever direction the wind takes it; hence, it can never blend in unnoticed. Science will not allow it. It all comes down to physics. And although it might seem complex and confusing at first glance, it's quite simple really: You cannot possibly understand the physics of The Game if you don't understand the mathematics of the movement. As ambiguous as this may seem for some, there are those who get it.

Math is science. It all comes down to the simple solution of adding and subtracting, hence is the term "Do the math." Just as science is the knowledge or study of the natural world based on facts learned through experiment and observation, the same method is used in The Game by incorporating formulas that are known to produce particular results.

What it comes down to is this: Keep it simple! Many people are fascinated by chaos and complexity so they're intrigued by rhetoric. Just because someone says they are a player, does not mean he is. Do the math! If there is an individual who is not practicing the principles of a player then it is evident he is not who he says he is. And in retrospect, if *you* are not demonstrating the characteristics that emulate a participant of The Lifestyle, chances are that, neither are you....

So, like I instructed earlier in this epistle, take a good look at yourself and inspect every intricate detail of what the fuck you're doing. If you don't like what you see when you look at yourself in the mirror; you don't have to be a science major to understand the physics of this truth: Neither will anyone else!

GET YOUR SHIT TOGETHER!

You cannot remedy anything by condemning it! – Mac BAS

Let's talk about where you are right now in The Game and go backward to understand how you got here – a moment of introspection, if you will.

What are your true aspirations in The Game? What are your personal goals and objectives? What do you wish to accomplish? What are you currently doing to reach your goals? Where do you see yourself in five years from now? And don't just give answers that you think sound good. If your answers are contradictory, then they're just mere words without meaning.

More often than not, the answers in our head can confuse us more than they can help us. This is not necessarily a bad thing. It's simply a conundrum because your goals are not realistic.

Discuss your ideas with other players around you and listen to their reactions. When we actually hear what others have to say, we often realize that our beliefs and opinions are not as insightful or valid as we may have convinced ourselves to believe; hence, we need to revise our plan by realistically assessing the situation.

Do not misinterpret my message! I'm not insinuating that you should allow others to discourage you or persuade you to believe that your goal (or goals) is not worthy to pursue. What I'm conveying is that you need to keep it real with yourself. We are responsible for shaping our own lives, so we must understand how to use our minds, what our values are, and in what way we incorporate these values into our plan.

So this brings me to ask: What are the core values at the root of your opinions? What are your personal beliefs? Why do you believe what you say you believe?

There is so much more involved with being an actual player of The Game besides just saying you are, thinking you are, portraying an image as if you are or wanting to be one. Just because someone is *playing the roll* does not constitute one as an actual participant of The Lifestyle. How can one claim to be a participant of something when they are oblivious of the inner dynamics of what they claim to be a part of?

Personally, I find it absolutely ridiculous when I see these imbeciles claiming to be players, yet do nothing beneficial to emulate the standards and expectations that epitomize the image that admirably represents The Game. At this point in my epistle, this fact should be clear.

Image is everything. Anyone that tells you it isn't is either an imposter, or in denial. There are schmucks whom have their priorities so grotesquely misplaced; they have tarnished their image as a result of their scandalous misdeeds and malicious intentions. And, unfortunately for them, The Game does not employ public relation specialists whom execute damage control campaigns to help salvage what little reputation they may have left.

For any of you up-and-coming players whom genuinely aspire to pave your path in The Game, I warn you: Beware of these imposters that are lurking within the realm of The Lifestyle like that of carp and catfish in rivers. These bottom-feeders are the player haters! They serve no purpose other than living off other players' reputations, interfering in player interactions, disrupting the rhythm of a player's flow, and undermining the hard work and efforts of a player's relentless pursuit of prosperity within The Game.

There is a zero-tolerance policy for those whom have been charged, tried, and convicted of being an imposter. Any obstacle in the midst of a player's path is to get knocked down and ran over. We do not waste time negotiating, nor do we compromise with those whom have infiltrated our society and demonstrated deliberate acts against a player with intentions of causing harm for his own insidious means.

With all that said, surely understood and out the way, I'm more interested in looking forward than looking backward. However, given the magnitude of challenges we've faced over the past decade, it is imperative for all players (including those whom believe they are) to do their own individual part and analyze all aspects of their character, so that they can polish the areas that need to shine, and sharpen the points of their plan that may have dulled.

Failure is not an option. The Game is going to exist with or without you. Therefore, get your shit together so that you can adapt to the existing circumstances.

I realize that many of you are not envisioning long-term. You can't find temporary solutions for permanent problems. When you encounter a dilemma, find a way to fix it, resolve your differences and move past it. When you leave issues unresolved you are allowing roadblocks to hinder your personal growth and development. The only person who will eventually suffer as a result of this, is you.

Remember, you cannot remedy anything by condemning

it! You only add to destructive patterns already permeating the atmosphere of your life. Get your shit together!

I'm here to move the wool that has been obstructing your view of the road to success from over your damn eyes. There are an enormous amount of individuals whom have been deceived and led to believe certain things about The Game that just simply aren't true. Most young men gravitate toward The Game with the right intentions, eager to learn the operations that are proven methods of increasing one's potential for advancement within The Game; however, they meet unfortunate circumstances early in The Game and encounter an imposter whose guidance they are more than willing to follow, hence, they are taught false ideals, provided inaccurate information, and are basically programmed to fail.

The only thing that anyone can learn from failure is what *not* to do. The ways of an imposter is the equivalent of false advertisement. Advertisers are powerful enough to tell people what to buy, what to look at, what to think, what to do, how to feel and what to believe. It's complete insanity because it's all done under false pretense.

There are few things which tell us how to be an independent thinker, how to be innovative, how to be creative, how to be business like, how to be successful. For that type of information we have to do our homework and become extremely disciplined.

Don't give in to obstacles. You persevere through failure by persisting through the rough times, constructing from criticisms, and learning from mistakes. When we make a mistake, we eliminate one more wrong way of doing something, hence, we move one step closer to what we wish to achieve.

It is a tremendous sorrow when one discovers the beliefs he was programmed to cherish and adhere to are actually false. It is an even greater shame when, upon learning the truth, one chooses to continue living that lie. I refer to that as "internal dishonesty." Do you know what that means?

For those whom are infected by this mental parasite, I have a message for you: You are a liar! It is not the problem that you tell the lie, but that you actually think the lie. It's not just to make others like you, or to impress them; you are trying to impress yourself, because you do not like yourself. You have to understand that I know a lot about you, and I have taught all those whom I have mentored to recognize you by way of your scandalous nature. We know the real you. You can no longer hide behind the cloak of facáde you've created.

Your character flaws are transparent. What you fail to realize is that you are only annihilating your own reputation. If you treated someone as bad as you treat yourself, you would be guilty of a senseless murder, because ultimately, that is what you constantly do to your character. You commit premeditated murder to your repertoire, over and over again, perpetually murdering your image! You construct a complete fabrication of reality which is catastrophic in proportion. Your days are numbered; there is no room for muthafuckas like you in The Game.

So, for all those whom this description fits, this epistle is your proof of service of summons. The Game has divorced you based on irreconcilable differences, incurable insanity, unsound mind, fraud, and physical incapacity. With this understood, you shall do one of the following: Step back and turn your player pass in voluntarily; be pushed back as a result of your intentional infractions that have warranted the revocation of your Playboy privileges; or be forced back by way of any means necessary.

The choice is yours. Choose wisely. Keep in mind that, when you don't choose, you're choosing; you're choosing not to make a choice! So put your choosing shoes on and do it movin', ya bitch. YOU KNOW WHO YOU ARE!

There has been enormous progress in The Game over the last five years. In fact, I've witnessed first-hand more progress within the past five or six years than in all the years prior. That is what motivates me and makes me more determined to do all in my power to tighten up the perimeter of The Game and oust all the imposters who have absolutely no business in The Bidness.

To all the players in The Game who are out there on the field putting up those points on the score board; it is an immense honor knowing that there are those whom share my vision and understand that our lifestyle is not to be played with.

The universal language that everyone seems to understand is violence; hence, there are times wherein that is our only remedy. I lead by way of example and teach it how I preach it, thus I often encounter situations wherein I have to rearrange a muthafucka's face plate. It's unfortunate that there are so many schmucks who truly don't get it until they wake up two months later, twenty pounds lighter, with breathing tubes up their nostrils, catheter all up in their urinary tract and wondering where the fuck they're at. You were in purgatory, bitch! Your soul was set free as a result of your assumption that you could play with The Game!

It's a travesty when it has to go to that extreme in order to demonstrate the zero-tolerance policy for major violations of the player procedures. There are consequences for misrepresenting the nature of the policy. Literally and figuratively....

HOLLYWOOD EXTRAS

So I say to you; do not be bamboozled by those whom identify themselves as players and attempt to convince you of their authenticity. – Mac BAS

The Game is not a system made up of morals. We are a society of players whom work together toward common interests, beliefs and goals. The title of Player should be held in high regard. There are certain expectations and high standards that come with the commitment one makes when he decides to become a participant of The Lifestyle. When you are acknowledged as a true player, it means that, as an individual, you have the ability to stand on your own two, possess quality character, are a man of integrity, share similar beliefs as those whom live by the principles and policies of The Game, and over-all have what it takes to make the cut.

Nobody can just say that he's a player and expect to be

taken seriously. There are proper procedures established that one must follow when seeking to enter the realm of The Game. Keep in mind that nobody can approach an individual and ask if they would like to be a player. It does not operate on that component. Not even sometimes. So if you assumed it did, you're wrong. This is not for just anyone.

Think about it. Let's say, for example, there is a well-established, successful club that everyone wants to get into because it's reputation for extravaganza is impeccable. You will never see employees of this entity coming out and approaching "non-entities" with open invitations to just come on in. It does not work like that in real life. In fact, you would not even be able to get in if you stood in line. You have to make reservations in advance, get on the VIP list, and appreciate the privilege to rendezvous with the crowd everyone wants to rub elbows with. Make sense? It's logical. You have to think logically. Don't allow yourself to hold onto assumptions. The Game does not rely on common sense. It operates by way of logic; practical and sound judgment.

I have often inquired about and challenged people's fundamental beliefs, and I've noticed the way in which the majority make efforts to hold on to their assumptions even when there is no solid foundation or logic that supports what they say they believe.

People tend not to listen when they are confronted about their opinions which they have always regarded as their true convictions. On many occasions when I've engaged in dialogue regarding issues which hold relevance and contradict contemporary thinking, most prefer to remain in denial rather than learn something. Even when a person has evidently lost the debate (if that's what you want to call it), they would rather hold on to their opinion instead of becoming educated about something powerful and reasonable.

I've never been one to succumb to people's opinions, especially when they are based solely on assumptions. Everyone has one regarding every topic, so it's senseless to rely on perspectives that accommodate what someone assumes. An educated explanation will always rule over opinions people have as a result of being *told* to think a certain way. There is a difference between being defensive and defending. Being defensive comes by way of not being too sure. When you are defending, you are standing firm in your beliefs. When you continue to be defensive for the things you should be defending, and vice versa, it will be detrimental to your development.

There comes a point in a man's life when he realizes that he must change his pattern of perception and learn by way of his shortcomings. A person's strength will continue to be tested and challenged. That's the way life is.

I'm articulating this so you understand something crucial. If you have dilemmas that make it arduous for you in everyday life, you most certainly don't belong anywhere within the grit and grind of The Game. And this is not necessarily a bad thing. It simply means that the going-ons of The Game are not for you.

So, what should you do? Well, that's entirely up to you. I won't pretend as if I'm concerned about what the fuck you do. My sole concern is The Game. Anyone outside of it is irrelevant to me.

The only thing I can say that will possibly provide some comfort to your bruised ego is that you are definitely not alone. In fact, I'd realistically estimate that there are thousands of schmucks just like you who have misinterpreted the terms and conditions of the company contract; thus, their service is being terminated!

It makes absolutely no sense to me when someone says they are a player, when in fact, they can't comprehend the dynamics of The Game. It's impossible to understand the fundamentals of anything if you're on the sidelines seeing it only in a partial and impractical way.

To give a clearer perception of what I'm conveying; for instance, if someone is not familiar with the game of football, then when watching a game it may appear to be just a bunch of guys in leotards, bulky pads and helmets, chasing the guy who's holding the ball so they can violently knock him down. However, if you actually watch football for a while, you will begin to recognize what is actually occurring. You will see there is a plan at work in a system involved with laws and guidelines that actually influence the schematics of how it works.

Fans of football understand the nature of the sport and can provide their educated knowledge about what's happening based on their understanding of the essentials of football. When these fans first began watching football and weren't familiar with the fundamentals, however; they, too, may have saw it as sporadic, unsystematic activity with no true purpose. I myself am not a real fan of football, or any other sport for that matter, except for maybe boxing and Mixed Martial Arts, but nonetheless I can appreciate the nature of the sport because I have accumulated the knowledge and I understand the synthesis of the laws that govern the game.

This brings me to another topic that needs to be addressed. I am flabbergasted when I see these pathetic specimens running around with tattoos that symbolize certain aspects of The Game, when in fact they're incapable of qualifying to enter the beginning phase of any category pertaining to the quintessence of a player.

Tattoos don't mean a damn thing if there is no purpose behind them. It's the same thing as putting a nice paint job on a car that has rust and rot underneath it. It may cover it for a certain period of time, but eventually the decomposition of decay will surface and reveal what's really underneath the paint. A paint job does not have the ability to increase the efficiency of a car's performance.

I say this to emphasize something of importance: If you have a tattoo that is contrary to the image you emulate, cover it with something that best suits you because you will eventually encounter participants of the lifestyle, such as myself, whom find it extremely disrespectful and insulting when imposters violate the policy and false advertise.

For instance, if a schmuck has the Playboy bunny tattooed on him and claims to be affiliated with players of The Game, yet he is doing absolutely nothing to exemplify the high standards of The Game, that putz is committing trademark infringement!

So I say to you; Do not be bamboozled by those whom identify themselves as players and attempt to convince you of their authenticity by way of their mouths and markings that are, in fact, contrary to who they truly are. I consider these types of imposters as "Hollywood Extras" who remain safe on the sidelines like that of cheerleaders with pom-poms in their hands, cheering on the players whom are out there on the field doing their part like they're supposed to in order to make it happen.

Inevitably, there will always be those cowardly fanatics of The Game whom are fascinated by the fame and frenzy of our lifestyle, yet are not willing to step out of their comfort zones and risk putting themselves in harm's way. Rather than working hard to develop the essential fundamentals that shape and hone one's skills, they prefer perfecting their art of acting. Their tattoos are merely that of "Hollywood makeup" that the "visual performance artists" wear to enhance the character they portray.

This brings up a very important factor in all this; as players, you have the right to confront these unresolved contradictions because it is your responsibility to expose the infiltrators who are not applying the correct methods of our principles which work to move us forward within The Game. Do not enable these impersonators by condoning their shenanigans!

The core of our society is deeply and firmly rooted in such a way that indoctrinates and inculcates certain dynamics that can't be forged nor duplicated, hence, it is not arduous to recognize those whom are "Hollywood Extras" and serve no true purpose within the realm of The Game.

VISUALIZING SUCCESS

If you follow these instructions accordingly, you will plant in your mind the key ingredients of success in The Game.

– Mac BAS

My intentions have never been to find the most people, but more so to inspire the right people. It was no ordinary determination that surmounted the enormous hurdles of battle, disappointment, danger, discouragement, and the constant odds stacked against me; however, I persisted through the many perilous predicaments and achieved prosperity within the complexities of The Game, not outside of it.

My overall objective is to inculcate the organizing principles of success into the minds of all players of The Lifestyle, so they too can thrive and attain their goals by practicing the philosophy of The Game properly and effectively. Remember; we all have a significant function we must regulate. Do so with persistence and consistency so that you shall have the ability to perceive the inconsistencies. Shall you choose to neglect your responsibilities and allow these imposters to demonstrate behavior that does not define the quintessential fundamentals of a player, then you, too, are guilty of aiding and abetting these conscious and deliberate acts which plague our environment, and spread the infestation of their mental disease that incapacitates the abilities needed to participate in the interactions of The Game.

Every choice in life is a calculation. Many of the choices people make derive from benefit analysis – what they believe is best for them. Sometimes you may calculate that it is in your best interest to avoid doing something that brings risks that may result in adverse effects. That is where miscalculation comes in. We each have lists of qualities that we look for which meet our expectations. Those whose have low expectations have a tendency of seeing something good in everyone they meet because it doesn't require much to qualify the standards of low expectations.

Now, for those of us whom expectations are that of a high level, we have standards that aren't easily met or satisfied, hence, we are not impressed nor captivated by those whom have minimal qualities. So I say to you holders of standards which are on that of a lower level; Raise the bar! It does not matter how we wish things were, it matters how we deal with the way they are. Learn to develop resilience. Strengthen the dynamics which maximize your potential. The Game is an aggregation of commitment by all true players to uphold their part of the agreement to maintain the integrity of The Lifestyle.

When you change the way you look at people, the people you look at change. You are most powerful when you keep it real with yourself. Don't allow people to pretend to be players when you know they are not.

Confidence and direction; I can't give you that. I can only give you the guidance that contributes to this. The confidence has to come from within. Know what you know, and know what you don't know. Having integrity means that you are honest with yourself and can say something and mean it – that you can make a commitment and stick to it.

Many people prefer to remain in predictable situations that are safe. When you start making significant changes, it catapults a chain reaction to making more changes that are necessary to elevate your game. When you have inner confidence, you can speak your thoughts and be in control of your voice because you're confident in what you're thinking.

In the event you encounter a dilemma that you cannot

resolve on your own, seek advice from a player who can assist you, then shut the fuck up and listen to what he has to say. Geniuses know how to prevent problems before they happen, smart people know how to solve them once they've occurred, and stupid muthafuckas think they have it all figured out, yet continue making the same mistake over and over again while expecting a different result. Some call it insanity. I call it being a stupid muthafucka!

This is that of an instruction manual. If you follow these instructions accordingly, you will plant in your mind the key ingredients of success in The Game. Repetition builds reflex. By repeating this procedure, you create a thought process that can in fact work in your favor.

It baffles me how much effort some people make to create false images of who they are for no reason other than to build a believable persona that will have them acknowledged as a player. If they used the same effort toward accumulating the monetary equivalent, they'd be rich!

There is a well-known saying that "knowledge is power." I believe that is complete bullshit, and here's why: knowledge will not amount to anything if you don't know how to apply it to whatever you're doing. What good is having knowledge if you don't actually understand it?

Knowledge is information. Period. What you do with that

information may or may not increase your potential in whatever you wish to achieve, but simply knowing something doesn't amount to shit unless you know what the fuck to do with it.

I'm mentioning this for a reason. Realistically, the wisdom I'm sharing with you will not produce appreciable results by merely reading what I'm illustrating. There must first be an inner desire already resonating from within in order to connect to the influencing source of understanding. You cannot possibly apply any of these principles with persistence if you lack ambition. There is nothing I can do to make you ambitious. If anyone ever tells you that they have methods that can make you ambitious, slap that son of a bitch across the face because he's a muthafuckin' liar!

Although there are proven formulas to success, ambition comes from an inner desire to succeed. The only person who can control that, is you. If you try and fail, it certainly cannot be the formula's fault, because it's already been proven! The fault is on the individual!

Success requires persistence; so keep on trying until you succeed. Concentrate on the goal you wish to accomplish, and envision already having accomplished it. I'm not insinuating to "think it into existence" because I don't believe in all that bullshit. If that's the type of shit you're into, put this epistle down and go read 'The Secret', or some other bullshit that might suit your fancy, because you're delusional if you believe you can just close your damn eyes and something of importance will manifest.

Look; What I'm describing to you is "visualizing success" so that your inspiration is triggered. Then, put your plan into action and persist until you succeed!

The mere fact that you are seeking knowledge is an indication that you're headed in the right direction. What you do with this knowledge, however, is completely up to you. If you have intentions of using this advanced knowledge with malice toward other players, you are destined to fail! Success in The Game comes by way of cooperation. It is necessary to work with other participants of The Lifestyle who are performing the correct way. And although every player has his own unique way of performing his plan, we all have goals which are similar in nature, so as long as a player is not blocking your path, stay in your lane as well and don't interfere with his performance.

Direct your attention to what it is that *you* want to achieve. Educate yourself in all areas pertaining to what you wish to accomplish, and never stop accumulating knowledge. As you acquire information, put it to use so that it serves its purpose. What good is having knowledge in a specific area if you're not applying it?

You don't have to be the smartest, most intellectual person to be successful. I know many individuals whom attained success, yet are far from the brightest of people I've met. What they had in their favor, however, was the inner drive to keep trying until they found their calling, and once they realized what they were good at, they focused their energy on acquiring knowledge related to their profession. The stupid muthafuckas are those who think they are good at everything. Jacks of all trades become masters of nothing.

THE PLAYER PROCESS

What I'm emphasizing is that there is only one way to go about being considered a true player. – Mac BAS

Just as there are many different areas of expertise in any corporation, there are many different genres of The Game. Watch this; let's talk football again for a moment as to give you a mental visual of what I'm indicating. A team is made up of players who have expertise in certain areas that are required to fulfill a role that's required to give it that winning edge. There is a quarterback, linebacker, running back, fullback, safety, wide receiver, offensive and defensive line, etc. Every player has a significant role to play; hence, his responsibility is equally important as the rest of the team's. Just because a person may be a damn good quarterback does not necessarily mean that he has the ability to fill the role of a linebacker, and vice versa. The first-string lineups are the starters because they have the ability to play their part with the most efficiency. But that does not mean the second and third string are less important, because they too possess a particular set of skills but have yet to develop their peak potential. Shit, even a water boy has his specific role to play that makes him part of the team. In fact, there are some water boys who have been with a certain team longer than many of the players. Why? Because he takes his role seriously and is great at what he does.

What genre of the game do you specialize in?

Having game does not classify you as being in The Game. Just like having a couple narrow-minded females on the team does not make you a player. Being a player requires more aptitude than attitude. The true definition of a player is one whom has made exceptional progress within the elements of a specific genre of The Game, and one who lives his life by the code of The Lifestyle.

The only way that one can be acknowledged as a true player in The Game is by following the concepts of the player process:

1) Seek participation in the interactions within the realm of The Game. 2) Attain sponsorship by two or more factors of The Game. 3) Understand the established ramifications once being officially embraced into The Game by one's peers of

players. 4) Attain mentorship by an educated player whom can teach the BASic Fundamentals of The Game.

If you identify yourself as a player yet have done none of the aforementioned, you will be discredited and forced to forfeit your place in The Game until you have completed the player process.

What I'm emphasizing is that there is only one way to go about being considered a true player. The Game will force nothing upon anyone; however, in retrospect, it expects everything of everyone whom is a participant of our movement. By following the instructions I'm emphasizing, you will circumvent possible disaster. The great players of The Game become great because they developed the faculties of their ambition and inner desire to succeed.

Those whom appropriate an identity to perpetrate an image will be much easier to identify once more players become educated by their experiences and learn the proper and practical way of representing our society. There is an abundant amount of opportunity for those whom are loyally devoted to The Game. For those disloyal imposters whom knowingly create false images in order to facilitate their impersonation, pay very close attention to what I'm about to emphasize: You lack purpose in life as a result of your character deficiency. There is no hope for you to ever succeed in my lifestyle. You lack ambition and will never amount to anything other than a failure. The Game defecates on your mediocrity and puts your pathetic persona in a permanent state of paralysis. You are merely a photo bomber who lives in the shadow of those who know your true identity. You are perpetually positioned in the fetal frame of failures who blame everyone else for their misery. You're all too eager to quit at the first sign of a challenge. You are what we call in The Game, "bitch made." I bet if you count your ribs, you have an extra one. You are the way you are because it's in your nature. Chances are very likely that you come from a family of failures. You've been cloned from a long line of losers, ya bitch.

You see, people will normally act on impulse when faced with having to make a decision, so if it's their instinct to quit whenever faced with adversity, they are doing what's in their nature, thus, there is nothing that you or anyone else can do to change that. It's the law of nature that causes things to do what they do. You don't have to teach a dog to bark; it will bark on its own because it's meant to do so. If a person has a loser's instinct, it's in their nature to tap out under pressure. The Game has an interminable rear-naked choke hold on the malicious maneuvers of imposters; hence, any effort made to succeed in The Game will be rendered unconscious.

We often encounter contradictory schmucks who suffer

from "delusional grandeur." They've convinced themselves that the act, image, etc., they've manufactured, holds some sort of relevance. They don't have the ability to adequately distinguish their personal contradictions. As a player, it is your responsibility to judge these imposters who are oblivious of the consequences for their actions. Don't be one to conform to the conventional cliché that encourages the masses not to judge others. Those whom attempt to persuade you to disregard your sense of judgment toward others, normally have an ulterior motive for doing so and likely want to avoid being judged for his own contradictories and inconsistencies.

 I warn you to avoid misjudgments. It's easy to judge poorly. I've seen many individuals who put themselves in some very diabolical predicaments as a result of being too quick to judge irrationally.

 The most powerful components of rational judgment are facts and logic. Information is everything when gathering facts. Never just go off of something that someone tells you. Especially when it's regarding another player. No circumstances persist unaltered; thus, secondhand information constantly changes. Devote some time to generate ideas of what actually works. The best technique for avoiding misjudging is asking relevant questions that require elaborate details in their answers. Listen for any statements that violate truth about what you already know. Relentlessly press forward with logical precision and execute your role to judge for yourself in player business.

CRASH-TEST DUMMIES

One thing about these schmucks that makes them easy to recognize is that they have a propensity for surrounding themselves with other dummies.
— Mac BAS

Everyone has been programmed a certain way. Depending on the way you were raised, schooled; your social environments and experiences; many of your opinions and ideas stem from wanting to be accepted, or conforming to idealology that you were made to accept as truth.

Acceptance is not a bad thing. A sense of belonging is something that resonates within everyone. However, do not let this cause you to become susceptible to vulnerability!

You don't necessarily need to challenge everything, but you should always think things through. Don't be so quick to agree with something just because it sounds favorable.

Self-examine your beliefs and explore ways to cultivate a more critical and skeptical approach when it comes to your judgment. Think about how many people you know who have very strong opinions about everything, yet have never examined the root of their beliefs. These are the uneducated geniuses whom are fascinated by the latest media hype. They have all the answers to every problem. Let them tell it and you'll hear an outlandish solution to save the world!

Do not be one who entertains any of that mumbo jumbo. Know your part so you can focus on contributing your efforts where most needed.

Many players have the right intentions, but have never had the opportunity to find their place within The Game. Well, here it is! I'm providing this miraculous missive to the masses to entice that momentum to join in this campaign to penetrate the shadow of illusion that corrupts our society. If you are reading this, you are responsible for spreading this message. I'm not trying to change the world; I'm changing The Game! Let's go block to block, ghetto to ghetto, city to city, state to state and player to player so that it catapults a chain reaction that reaches across the nation!

Tradition becomes unwanted conviction. Many of you are living your lives according to how someone else thinks you should without you even being aware of it. Your minds are filled with clichés, fabricated ideas and miscellaneous malarkey that has been handed down and embedded in your brain from those around you. Never say never; It is what it is; Better safe than sorry; Good things come to those who wait; Good things happen to good people; Don't pay it back, pay it forward; blah, blah, blah. All you have to do is ponder these popular, preposterous phrases and you'll be able to identify other phrases that are equally popular, yet contrary to the message.

I say to reconsider living your life based on selected perspectives of those who don't truly emulate the dynamics of a player. If you analyze the aspects of an imposter's attitude, beliefs and points of view, you'll recognize that most of what he expresses comes from his heavy indulgence of newspapers, radio, television and magazines. They get their game from listening to rap CDs and portray images that mimic their favorite rapper or actor.

A person like myself, raised and educated in all aspects of The Game, I realize that education is in fact the most effective and powerful tool in personal progress and development of individuals. So if you don't know the facts regarding a specific genre of The Game you're interested in; rather than venturing to conjecture, invest your time toward researching, studying and educating yourself.

There are many successful players whom serve as astounding examples of applied persistence. There are just as many, if not more, however, whom I'm sure you can recall that have accepted their failures as fate, or just having the worst of luck, when in fact, the truth is, they are always falling asleep at the wheel and they drive right past every opportunity that may've been presented had they been paying attention. Any form of creativity has been declared deceased; hence, they are in need of having a fuckin' defibrillator pressed against their head in attempt to resurrect their game from the god-damned dead! Innovation deficient muthafuckas. I'm quite certain that as you're reading this truth I'm articulating, there are several schmucks that come to mind. This class of individuals is categorized as Crash-Test Dummies.

I advise you to use caution when dealing with these imbeciles because every decision they make is based on a hunch. Running face first into iron gates comes naturally to their stupid asses because they keep their eyes closed in the midst of traffic. Ever hear about the idiots who spontaneously put their foot on the gas rather than the brake and run their vehicle into a storefront? Yeah, that's them! They have no business being behind the wheel, yet, unfortunately, they seem to always be the ones wanting to drive.

There is overwhelming evidence that supports the theory that most Crash-Test Dummies suffer from inferiority complex. The most common symptoms exhibited in those whom have this character ailment, is an overzealousness in their attempt to appear as if they have a sense of superiority by constantly lying about things they don't have, claiming to have accomplished goals they've never endeavored, and having a tendency to imitate the personalities of those around them who actually are what they just wish to be.

One thing about these schmucks that makes them easy to recognize is that they have a propensity for surrounding themselves with other Dummies. Stupid people enjoy the company of people even stupider than they are because it gives them a sense of adequacy. Ironically, smart people relish the company of counterparts whom are of equal or even greater intellect, and thrive on being introduced to new innovative ideas that enhance their potential to prosper.

FORMULATE YOUR GAME PLAN

Up your game so you can increase your potential for success. – Mac BAS

It is imperative to keep an eye peeled for the techniques of deception used by imitators. It is not difficult to identify because they can't help but indulge in their habitual behavior. They habitually fabricate stories for no apparent reason other than to impress others. They habitually get in other people's business that they have no business being involved in. They habitually make false promises concerning what they're going to have. They habitually speak negatively behind people's backs yet, while in the presence of these same individuals, they act as if they are elated!

True players never say anything behind anyone's back that they won't say to their face. If you don't like someone, never pretend as if you do. It's unnecessary, and only depreciates the value of your character.

You're not going to get along with every player you meet. Sometimes there are personality differences, character clashes, or certain things about another player that just rubs you the wrong way. Ninety percent of the time, those who you don't like, don't like you either. Nevertheless, that does not mean that the two of you cannot co-exist, or even combine forces in some areas.

If you prefer keeping your distance, that's entirely up to you, but never speak down on a player. If you do, it can be construed as you being a hater. No player wants to be referred to a term as derogatory as that of a hater. And remember, regardless of whom you may or may not like, you must keep in mind that all players share a common denominator that is bigger than us all: The Game!

As a player in The Game, you have the right to speak your mind, voice your opinions and involve yourself in player bidness, especially if it's a situation that can impact other players. When you have the honor of being regarded as a true player, it means that you have been approved, anointed and appointed. This only happens for qualified applicants. Your player pass is not activated until you've been officially elected into The Game.

In many cases a player will define his place in The Game as more so of a job than a way of life. Those who consider it a job tend to focus on the immediate prospects. Immediacy normally amounts to spontaneous and temporary, hence, is short-term the majority of the time. When seeing The Game as a lifestyle, you realize that it is a long-term commitment and your thinking is specifically directed toward longevity.

Those of us who have been in The Game for many years have the ability to identify the likeliest candidates whom meet all the specific requirements to be elected as a true player.

If whatever you are doing is working, then I commend you and encourage you to continue using your winning strategy while adopting my proven formula, to help improve your overall game plan in an effort to increase your success. Now, if for one reason or another your plan doesn't seem to be working, then simply contemplate your reason for doing what you're doing so you can draw a line of clarification as to why you are not achieving your goal. Many players have a tendency to settle for the first opportunity that comes their way, not realizing that there will be many more to follow. The determination to accomplish that goal hinders your ability to pursue other goals.

You need to prioritize in terms of rearranging your game plan. Determine what your goals are, and consider what options and resources are available to you.

Here is an example of how to formulate your plan and make significant changes in your strategy:

1) **R**eevaluate your game plan.

2) **E**xamine what progress you have made.

3) **D**etermine whether or not to proceed with the same goal or start another.

4) **I**ntrospect your thoughts and take a moment to reflect on your objectives.

5) **R**ealistically assess yourself by acknowledging the areas where you need to up your game so you can increase your potential for success.

THE RIGHT WAY

There is one right way of doing everything and many wrong ways.

– Mac BAS

There are many of those whom live their lives feeding on a heavy dose of propaganda that instills outlandish, unrealistic ideas into their minds which keeps them too deeply entrenched in their circumstances to prevail past the bullshit. Possessing opinions without principles, having miscellaneous information without facts and holding on to beliefs that are unfounded, will only push you further away from success and into an atmosphere of fraudulent representation which only contradicts your sense of identity.

Critically examine the axioms of the ideas and beliefs you've been holding onto so that you can perhaps let go of the binding bullshit that might be holding you back. All too often

I have encountered those whom have enormous potential to succeed in The Game, yet are hindered by their conventional beliefs that are invalid, irrelevant and untrue.

There is compelling reason behind the deeply rooted beliefs within The Game which are supported by unquestionable amount of evidence and experiences that lead true players' commitments to live by the code of The Lifestyle. When reflecting on your opinions and beliefs, you are going to have to conclude on your own judgment. If you detect errors, develop possible solutions to correct them and find more effective ways of gathering information that helps you enrich and deepen your understanding so that your opinionating skills are sound. Sharpening your mind will enable you to plan, prepare and perform properly when resolving issues. It's all about technique and tactic. Warrant your conclusions based on results that are consistent with the concepts of The Game; not contrary to it.

Players value the way in which they live, so there are always those whom are not only willing, but actually enjoy providing key elements that can assist other participants of The Game. We as a society benefit from meeting, socializing, networking and sharing exhilarating dialogue with other players whom can enhance and elevate our game so that we can generate the components that allow us to rise above the level of obstacles that we all shall eventually encounter along the way. Each one teach one is a common concept that all players practice and convey, hence, one should pay attention to alternative views and respond to conversation that hones and stimulates your mind's development in a way that allow fulfilling your potential.

In many ways the concepts of The Game are similar to a sum in mathematics. It may be bewilderingly arduous and complicated to those whom have yet to grasp the key to its solution, but once it is perceived and understood it becomes as enormously simple as it was previously profoundly perplexing.

Some idea of this relative simplicity and complexity of The Game may be fully grasped by recognizing the fact that while there are many ways in which a sum may be done wrong, there is only *one way* by which it can be done right. And that when the *right way* is found and the player knows it to be right, his perplexity vanishes and he knows he has mastered the problem.

There is one right way of doing everything and many wrong ways. Skill consists in finding the one right way and sticking to it. Don't misconstrue what the fuck I'm indicating here by assuming that I'm implying that everyone has to do the exact same thing when executing a particular plan. We all have our own way of doing things. What might work for others may not necessarily work for you. However, if what you're doing isn't working, then obviously you are going about it the wrong way.

You have to have insight to perceive the inner cause of failing to find a solution to whatever problem you're having. Be sure to stay away from those schmucks who, even when pointing it out to them, they still cannot see the right way. They're ignorant and assume that they know what's best, thereby placing themselves in situations where it becomes impossible to learn, even if it's learning something that can be beneficial to them.

Ignorance and inefficiency are all too common. The point I'm making is this; there are enormous opportunities in The Game for those whom are efficient. As a Mac, I know first-hand how difficult it can be to find a player who is best suited for the job. A certified player with credentials will *always* find a place or position in The Game to exercise his skills. A player's principle should include having ways to calm and clarify the mind so that one can focus their energy on manifesting greater skill, so it becomes more powerful and increases the potential to be effective and successful in a particular pursuit within The Game.

Remember: *an imposter cannot prosper!* Any move they make to gain leverage will inevitably collapse. But it is not only the imposter who may be doing things the wrong way! All those who are gaining or trying to gain leverage in The Game without giving the equivalent, is doing it wrong whether he is aware of it or not.

There are many young players who come into the game blind, rambunctious and oblivious of what is actually required. They are unable to gain proper perspective and develop an appreciation for responsibility. They're constantly scheming on how to get something without working for it. Don't be a fuckin' swindler! If you want to accumulate prosperity in The Game, you have to practice good old-fashion integrity. It will take you far. When you persistently press forward the right way, you will certainly reach a destination associated with *that* way.

And so I ask you to ask yourself; which direction are *you* headed? The wrong way or the *right* way!?

THE LAW OF THE GAME

"where-ever law ends, tyranny begins"
- John Locke

There is an established foundation of law within The Game that when violated, leads to failure. Ignorance of this law does not make you exempt, it only increases the probability of violating it.

All players are governed by the law of The Game. It exists to bring transparency and accountability to the going-ons and interaction of participants of The Lifestyle.

Compliance does not mean that everything is managed perfectly, but it does mean that all players have a BASic and functioning process to ensure that a well-informed discussion is happening. Compliance will ensure that all players are contributing to The Game's long-term development in one way or another.

I am a firm believer in stability. Sustained player commitment is needed to continue in the right direction. Together we have the potential to propel forward and have a significant impact within The Game.

Individually, all players must encourage and support participation and proper practices. If you have the resources, it's imperative for you to provide access to help facilitate the interactions of The Game, so that we can stay connected to a coherent network of players who are focused on taking things to an unprecedented level.

As players, it is your responsibility to demonstrate your commitment to the hard work necessary to accomplish the progress-minded goals, through improvement of the social interactions of The Game.

I'm using this book as a platform of opportunity to highlight the importance of educating yourself to the BASic fundamentals of The Game so that your participation and representation will help accelerate the social development, improve the outcome of a players endeavor, and strengthen the right governance.

The law of The Game is instituted for the protection and prosperity of all players. It comes into operation as a punishing factor when it is violated, thus offenders of it regard it with contempt and disdain. The law of The Game is that which protects and upholds. Those who violate it, either willfully or because of ignorance shall suffer the penalty of their wrong doing. But, to those who obey it; embrace it with exuberance and shall flourish. Law cannot be altered. The law of The Game is a method of justice.

The same law that punishes is the same law that preserves. Each and every mistake we have made has brought us one step closer to achieving our goal. We progress by learning and we learn by recognizing our mistakes. Success is assured to all those who perceive the law of The Game as the reigning regulating factor in their life and obey it. As I conveyed, the law of The Game cannot be altered, however, what we can do is alter ourselves as to better understand the BASic fundamentals of The Game so that we can perceive the truth that exists in applying the method of obedience.

The fundamentals are BASic principles. You will avoid confusion by thoroughly learning how to apply them to the details of your life so that you can cultivate an invincible character. There can be no compromise of principles. The first principles of The Game are principles of conduct. You can't just say them and think you comprehend them. You must actually learn them, study them, and educate yourself to them so that you are then able to practice them efficiently. There are many principles. It is impossible for me to provide you with every principle that details every aspect of The Game, but I will elaborate on 5 of the BASics to provide some insight.

With the introduction of this regulating factor, you can perceive that certain habits must be abandoned in order to conduct yourself in accordance with the demands of an ideal. All players must adjust their minds to an ideal. Once you put it all in perspective you will be able to understand what actually constitutes a permanent principle.

1. Responsibility: A duty or task that you are required or expected to do.

2. Economy: The process or system by which goods or service are produced, sold and bought.

3. Determination: A quality that makes you continue trying to do or achieve something that is difficult.

4. Idealism: The attitude of a person who believes that it is possible to live according to very high standards of behavior and honesty.

5. Realism: The quality of a person who understands what is real and possible in a particular situation and is able to deal with it in a practical way.

Those who diligently practice and adhere to the above principles will develop the purpose and power which will enable him to successfully deal with every difficulty and surmount every obstacle with efficiency.

I don't like when muthafuckars site something and they don't know the substance. Don't be one of those stagnant muthafuckars who run off at their mouth about certain subjects, yet don't really know what the fuck they are talking about.

When you incorporate these principles into your repertoire you can practice them efficiently. Do not be one who suffers the delusion of believing his lapse of conduct is due to those around him. You and you alone are responsible for your own actions.

The law of The Game must be understood, applied and obeyed before true success can be attained. It is a necessity for all players to clearly perceive his wrongs so he can formulate a method of rectifying them. Having a process of remedying faults gives you the ability to cultivate and develop strengths which work to regulate a higher level of conduct in your performance of duty.

All players must regard their responsibilities with faithful adherence so that his actions are practical, acquired and comprehended accurately and according to law. Those who engage in deception and look for a personal advantage in everything they do are misrepresenting and violating the rules of conduct.

A true player does not indulge in deceptive tactics, trickery nor prejudice toward other players. To do so is a blatant disregard for the law of The Game.

Be true to your convictions. Do what you regard as right and do not procrastinate in carrying out serious measures in your performance of duty when you are certain that it is necessary. It is not necessary to be the best at everything. If you are doing the best you can, then you are performing your duty accordingly and will discover ways to increase your performance. As long as you are willing to learn you will continue to progress.

Contemplate, concentrate and cooperate prior to performing so that you do not hesitate in time of action. Dealing with difficulties produces power. Those who constantly follow the flow of least resistance because it's the easiest route will constantly remain weak, miserable and disappointed in their circumstances.

There is no shortcut to prosperity. The short-sighted muthafuckas who constantly look for the short cuts, undermine their character and impose on themselves. A true player will always do right by another player. His integrity and confidence commands the respect of those around him. There is a certain grandeur in the presence of all players, which inspires and motivates the influential power of rectitude. Imposters live in constant fear of their faulty character being exposed and having to face the consequences of those misdeeds, however, participants of The Lifestyle whom fulfills his obligations, honors his responsibilities and produces an admirable reputation, are fearless because he stands so firm in the invincibility of the law of The Game.

Author's Bio

MAC BAS is highly regarded as one of the most influential visionaries in The Game. He is a founder, philanthropist, lifestyle expert, motivational speaker, life coach, CEO, author, artist and poet. His innovation courage and determination propels him to succeed at all costs. He is a connoisseur in the field of self-development and committed to the prosperity of The Game.

THE CELL BLOCK
PRESENTS

THE INVITATION

WITHIN THE INNER REALM OF THE GAME

A Book By

MAC BAS

COMING SOON!

ALSO AVAILABLE!

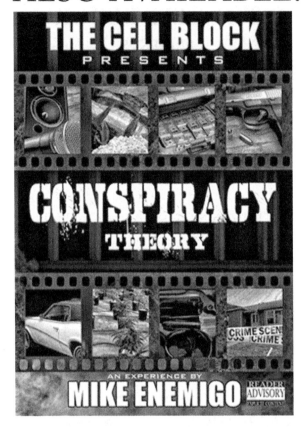

CONSPIRACY THEORY, $15.00 (* OR 2.5 BOOKS OF STAMPS): Kokain in an upcoming rapper trying to make a name for himself in the Sacramento, CA underground scene, and Nicki is his girlfriend. ... One night, in October, Nicki's brother, along with her brother's best friend, go to rob a house of its $100,000 marijuana crop. It goes wrong; shots are fired and a man is killed .... Later, as investigators begin closing in on Nicki's brother and his friend, they, along with the help of a few others, create a way to make Kokain take the fall .... The conspiracy begins.

* All stamps must be new, complete books of 20 forever stamps. You may include half books of new, forever stamps, where they are required.

THE CELL BLOCK · PO BOX 212 · FOLSOM, CA 95763
PRICES ARE SUBJECT TO CHANGE.

ALSO AVAILABLE!

THEE ENEMY OF THE STATE (SPECIAL EDITION), $9.99 (* OR 1.5 BOOKS OF STAMPS): Experience the inspirational journey of a kid who was introduced to the art of rapping in 1993, struggled between his dream of becoming a professional rapper and the reality of the streets, and was finally offered a recording deal in 1999, only to be arrested minutes later and eventually sentenced to life in prison .... However, despite his harsh reality, he dedicated himself to hip-hop once again, and with resilience and determination, he sets out to prove he may just be one of the dopest rhyme writers/spitters ever .... At this point, it becomes deeper than rap .... Welcome to a preview of the greatest story you never heard.

* All stamps must be new, complete books of 20 forever stamps. You may include half books of new, forever stamps, where they are required.

THE CELL BLOCK · PO BOX 212 · FOLSOM, CA 95763
PRICES ARE SUBJECT TO CHANGE

ALSO AVAILABLE!

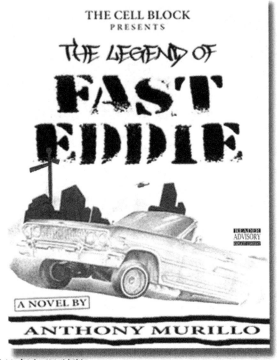

tHE URBAN CULT CLASSIC IS BACK!

FAST EDDIE, $15.00 (OR 2.5 BOOKS OF STAMPS): Originally published as Wicked Sick nearly a decade ago, The Legend of Fast Eddie is a nail biting joyride through the treacherous world of organized crime... It's the summer of 2003. A routine carjacking turns into the come-up of a lifetime when a young cholo from East L.A. accidently intercepts a large heroin shipment. Soon, a number of outlaw groups, including the notorious Mexican Mafia, is hot on his trail. As a bloody free-for-all ensues, some events are captured on video and posted online by a sadistic assassin dispatched by the dope's true owner. Hundreds of snuff flick enthusiast watch in real time as the deadly cast of characters fight to come out on top. In the end, only one can win. For the rest, it will be Game Over.

* All stamps must be new, complete books of 20 forever stamps. You may include half books of new, forever stamps, where they are required.

THE CELL BLOCK · PO BOX 212 · FOLSOM, CA 95763

PRICES ARE SUBJECT TO CHANGE.

ALSO AVAILABLE!

KANO'S STRUGGLE, 15.00 (OR 2.5 BOOKS OF STAMPS): Like most kids growing up in the hood, Kano has a dream of going from rags to riches. But when his plan to get fast money by robbing the local "mom and pop" shop goes wrong, he quickly finds himself sentenced to serious prison time. Follow Kano's struggle as he is schooled to the ways of the game by some of the most respected OGs who ever did it; then is set free and given the resources to put his schooling into action and builds the ultimate hood empire...

* All stamps must be new, complete books of 20 forever stamps. You may include half books of new, forever stamps, where they are required.

THE CELL BLOCK·PO BOX 212·FOLSOM, CA 95763

PRICES ARE SUBJECT TO CHANGE.

ALSO AVAILABLE!

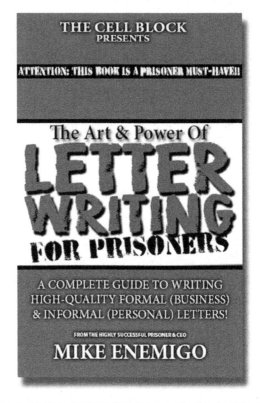

THE ART & POWER OF LETTER WRITING FOR PRISONERS, $9.99 (* OR 1.5 BOOK OF STAMPS): When locked inside a prison cell, being able to write well is the most powerful skill you can have! Learn how to increase your power by writing high-quality personal and formal letters! Includes letter templates, pen-pal website strategies, punctuation guide and more!

* All stamps must be new, complete books of 20 forever stamps. You may include half books of new, forever stamps, where they are required.

THE CELL BLOCK · PO BOX 212 · FOLSOM, CA 95763

PRICES ARE SUBJECT TO CHANGE.

ALSO AVAILABLE!

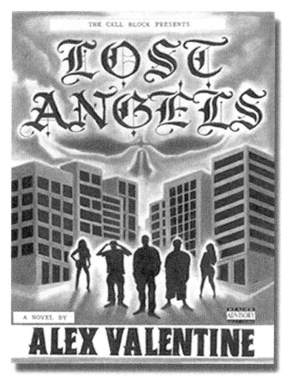

LOST ANGELS, $15.00 (OR 2.5 BOOKS OF STAMPS): "David Rodrigo was a child who belonged to no world; rejected for his mixed heritage by most of his family and raised by an outcast uncle in the mean streets of East L.A. Chance cast him into a far darker and more devious pit of intrigue that stretched from the basest gutters to the halls of power in the great city. Now, to survive the clash of lethal forces arrayed about him, and to protect those he loves, he has only two allies; his quick wits, and the flashing blade that earned young David the street name, Viper."

* All stamps must be new, complete books of 20 forever stamps. You may include half books of new, forever stamps, where they are required.

THE CELL BLOCK·PO BOX 212·FOLSOM, CA 95763

PRICES ARE SUBJECT TO CHANGE.

ALSO AVAILABLE!

LOYALTY AND BETRAYAL, $12.00 (* OR 2 BOOKS OF STAMPS):
Chunky was an associate of and soldier for the notorious Mexican Mafia -- La Eme. That is, of course, until he was betrayed by those he was most loyal to. Then he vowed to become their worst enemy. And though they've attempted to kill him numerous times, he still to this day is running around making a mockery of their organization .... This is the story of how it all began.

* All stamps must be new, complete books of 20 forever stamps. You may include half books of new, forever stamps, where they are required.

THE CELL BLOCK · PO BOX 212 · FOLSOM, CA 95763

PRICES ARE SUBJECT TO CHANGE.

ALSO AVAILABLE!

THE BEST RESOURCE DIRECTORY FOR PRISONERS, $19.99 (* OR 3 BOOKS OF STAMPS): This book has over 1,550 resources for prisoners! Anything you can think of doing from your prison cell, this book has the resources to do it! Includes: 150+ pro bono attorneys, 130+ free pen pal clubs, free books and other publications, non-nude photo sellers, prisoner advocates, prisoner assistants, correspondence education, money-making opportunities; resources for prison artists, writers, poets, and much, much more! Increase your resources, increase your network, and increase your power!

THE CELL BLOCK·PO BOX 212·FOLSOM, CA 95763

All stamps must be new, complete books of 20 forever stamps. You may include half books of new, forever stamps, where they are required.

ALL PRICES ARE SUBJECT TO CHANGE.

Made in the USA
Las Vegas, NV
23 February 2021